THIS BOOK SHOULD BE RETURNED ON OR BEFORE THE LATEST
DATE SHOWN TO THE LIBRARY FROM WHICH IT WAS BORROWED

MOBILE

30 SEP 1998

- 2 DEC 1998

22 FEB 1999

19 AUG 1999

RAWTENSTALL
5/00

03 JUN 2017

12 DEC 02

PG 18.11.03

25. NOV

11. DEC

03. JAN 01

3 0 DEC 2004

21. NOV 01

29 DEC 2006

BACUP

01. DEC 01 - 1 DEC 2010

25. NOV 02

3 0 NOV 2013

2 7 JUL 2013

2 2 DEC 2010

1 3 JAN 2004

AUTHOR	CLASS	Jt P1
HILL, E.	2 4 JAN 2014	christmas

TITLE

29 DEC 2014

Spot's magical Christmas

03 DEC 2014

RAWTENSTALL

Published by Ladybird Books Ltd Loughborough Leicestershire UK
A subsidiary of the Penguin Group. A Pearson Company

Printed in the United Kingdom by Ladybird Books Ltd – Loughborough

Spot's Magical Christmas

Eric Hill

Ladybird

It is Christmas
Eve, the day
before Christmas.
Spot is putting
a star on the
Christmas tree.

073821211

Oh dear!

Spot's mum, Sally, thinks Spot is too excited. She tells Spot to go out and play in the garden.

In the garden Spot sees his dad, Sam, lifting logs into a basket.

"I'm coming to help you, Dad," says Spot.

Suddenly Spot and Sam hear a voice. "Excuse me. Hello."

There are two reindeer looking at them over the fence.

"Have you seen a sleigh? A big red sleigh?" ask the reindeer.

The reindeer sing a song to Spot, telling how they have lost Santa's sleigh. Without it he will not be able to deliver his presents that night.

Spot feels sad. He watches the reindeer go off to search for the sleigh in the woods.

"Why don't you ask your friends if they have seen the sleigh?" says Sam.

So Spot runs to his friend Helen's house.

Helen is making Christmas cookies. She says she will help Spot to look for Santa's sleigh.

Spot goes to see his friend Tom. Tom is putting up Christmas decorations. But he says he will help Spot look for the sleigh.

Then Spot goes to see his friend Steve. Steve is wrapping up his presents. He says he will help Spot, too.

"Let's take my little blue sledge with us," says Steve.

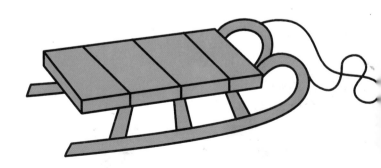

Spot, Helen, Tom and Steve go out in the snow to look for the sleigh.

Spot and Steve ride down the hill on Steve's sledge.

"Your sledge is great, Steve," says Spot. "I wish I had one just like it."

Then Tom and Helen have a ride on the sledge.

While they are gone, Spot and Steve collect a big pile of snowballs.

There is an exciting snowball
fight.

Everyone has fun but they
haven't found Santa's sleigh yet.

Spot and Steve have one last ride on the sledge. It goes faster and faster, and farther and farther, and doesn't stop until it is right among the trees.

"Look, Steve, look over there!" shouts Spot. "It's Santa's sleigh!"

"But it is getting late," says Helen, "and Santa needs his sleigh tonight. Go and ask your dad what to do, Spot."

Spot runs back home to his dad. "You must find the reindeer now," says Sam.

So Spot follows the reindeer's footprints in the snow, until he catches up with them.

The reindeer are very happy to hear that Spot has found the sleigh. "Would you like to have a ride in it before we take it back to Santa?" they say.

"I will ask Dad," says Spot.

"You may go for a ride in Santa's sleigh, Spot," says Sam. "But you mustn't be long."

"We'll be no time at all," the reindeer tell Sam. "Come on, Spot, let's go!"

Spot climbs into the sleigh and
they all set off. As the sleigh comes
out of the woods it rises up into
the air. The sky above is very dark
and full of stars. The reindeer
make the sleigh fly up in a big loop.

One star falls right beside the sleigh. Spot can almost touch it.

Then the sleigh flies off towards some mountains and into a cave in the rocks.

"It's Santa's workshop!" cries Spot, as he catches a bouncing ball.

Santa's teddy helpers are testing and packing toys. "Happy Christmas!" Spot calls to the teddies.

And then Santa appears from a gap in the rock and waves. "Ho, ho, ho! Happy Christmas, Spot!"

"It's time to go home now," say the reindeer.

The sleigh flies back over the mountains, through the stars and comes down at last beside Spot's house.

"Thank you, reindeer, that was wonderful," says Spot.

Indoors Spot tells his mum
and dad all about his adventure.
"Now you must hang up your
Christmas stocking," says Sally.
"I'll bring Santa's treats. He will
be here soon."

"I know, Mum," says Spot. "I think I'll go to bed now."

"Goodnight, Spot.
Sweet dreams."

And in the morning
there is one very special
extra present waiting
for Spot...